BENITO RUNS

JUSTINE FONTES

SURVIVING SOUTHSIDE

Benito Runs

Justine Fontes

darbycreek

MINNEAPOLIS

Darby Creek
A division of Lerner Publishing Group, Inc.
241 First Avenue North
Minneapolis, MN 55401 U.S.A.

Website address: www.lernerbooks.com

The images in this book are used with the permission of:
© Janine Wiedel Photolibrary/Alamy, (main image)
front cover; © iStockphoto.com/Jill Fromer, (banner
background) front cover and throughout interior;
© iStockphoto.com/Naphtalina, (brick wall background)
front cover and throughout interior.

Library of Congress Cataloging-in-Publication Data

Fontes, Justine.
    Benito runs / by Justine Fontes.
        p.   cm. — (Surviving Southside)
    ISBN: 978–0–7613–6151–0 (lib. bdg. : alk. paper)
    [1. Post–traumatic stress disorder—Fiction.
2. Fathers—Fiction. 3. Hispanic Americans—Fiction.]
I. Title.
PZ7.F73576Be 2011
[Fic]—dc22   2010023820

Manufactured in the United States of America
1 – BP – 12/31/10

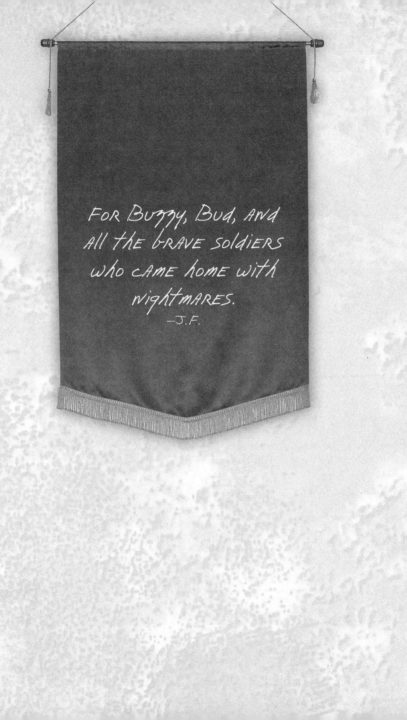

For Buzzy, Bud, and
all the brave soldiers
who came home with
nightmares.
—J.F.

CHAPTER 1

I hate writing. At least I used to. But believe me, if you ever feel like your life is falling apart, pick up a pen. It will help. I promise.

You probably don't believe me. I wouldn't have just a few months ago. I never liked writing papers for school or even letters.

I like to play soccer and hang out with my friends. I used to play soccer almost every day with my dad, Xavier. But that changed after he came home from Iraq.

Before the war, Dad used to sing all the time. And most weekends he'd cook. He used to make the best enchiladas!

Almost every weekend we did something fun, like go to a movie. Sometimes Dad would take the family bowling, even though he hated the ugly, striped shoes. He called them *zapatos feos*.

Mom, my younger sister Armida, and I didn't mind the shoes. They cracked us up. And if that didn't get us chuckling, we'd be laughing at each other, because we were all really bad at bowling. Watching the ball roll slowly into the gutter was always good for a laugh.

Once a month, Dad would go to National Guard camp. But it wasn't any big deal. While he was gone, Mom, Armi, and I would have fun. We'd eat pizza and stay up late watching TV. We liked doing all the things Dad wouldn't let us do if he was home.

Then, suddenly, Dad was told he was going to be deployed—into real combat! Mom and Armi freaked out. I did, too! But I didn't show it. With Dad heading to Iraq, he told me I would become the man of the house.

I tried to be a good leader. But it wasn't easy filling Dad's shoes. I'm not much of a singer. And I can barely boil an egg, much less make enchiladas. But I did my best to keep up morale.

Every Friday the three of us went bowling. It gave us something to look forward to.

Bowling was different without Dad. There was no one to complain about the *zapatos feos*. Mom seemed more like another kid than a parent. Armi and I teased her when she got a gutter ball. And she teased us back, instead of telling us to "play nice."

I had never thought of my mother as a person before. She was just Mom. But sometimes when she and Armi were giggling together they almost looked like sisters.

It freaked me out to realize that Mom had only been three years older than I was when she had met and married Dad. No way did I feel ready to become a parent! It was hard enough just being man of the house while Dad was away.

And I wasn't very strict. In Benito's *casa*, homework could wait until after soccer practice. Garbage could be bagged in the morning.

Bedtime became "whenever you fall asleep, wherever." Mom often fell asleep in front of the TV. I guess the chattering voices made her feel less alone.

While Dad was at boot camp, we missed him, but it wasn't that bad. Once he was actually in Iraq, things got scary. Dad was gone, and we realized he might not come back. Laughs became very precious. We bowled a lot of games trying to "soldier on" so that we didn't have to think about that.

Every week we mailed Dad a package. We tried to think of little things that he might miss from home and treats he could share with the other guys in his unit. We also sent lots of pictures.

Mom always nagged me, "Write him a letter." But I didn't know what to say. "Hi! How are you? I'm fine" didn't really cut it.

Dad wrote pretty often. Mom always read the letters silently to herself. Then she'd read them aloud to me and Armi. Sometimes her eyes filled with tears, and she'd get quiet for a while. I figured she was skipping the mushy parts. Although there was plenty of mushy stuff in the parts she read out loud.

Dad always wrote about how much he missed being with us. It was hard not to cry when Mom read that.

I missed Dad most at soccer time. Before supper, after homework, that used to be our time to play. We hadn't gone to the park or bothered with goal nets. We just kicked the ball around on the scrubby double lawn we share with the Joneses. They're the family in the other half of our attached house.

Steve Jones is my best friend. But he doesn't like soccer. Steve says, "That whole not-touching-the-ball-with-your-hands thing drives me crazy!" Steve's game is basketball.

I used to practice with my friend Dustin before he moved to Dallas. He used to live right up the street.

Most of the other soccer-squad guys stayed after school to practice. But I liked kicking the ball around at home with Dad and Dustin better.

With Dad gone, Steve tried to help. He played soccer with me a few times. But it wasn't the same.

Playing soccer with anyone else on that scrubby lawn just made me think of Dad. What if he died? What if he came home all messed up? What if he never came home and we never found out what happened to him?

After a while, I stopped kicking the ball around at all, except with the team at practice.

Then we found out that Dad was coming home! He'd be back in Texas in less than two weeks.

What a countdown! It was more intense than any Christmas or birthday. Dad was coming back, and everything was going to be great. We couldn't wait!

Mom went crazy cleaning up the house. Armi and I tried to help. But mostly we just tried to keep out of the way of Mom's humming vacuum cleaner.

Finally, there were thirteen Xs on the calendar. The great day had arrived! There wasn't a speck of dust left in the house. So Mom kept herself busy in the kitchen. She was cooking all of Dad's favorite foods.

Armi made a big "Welcome Home" banner. Steve and I helped her hang it up over the couch.

It was sagging in the middle, so Steve jumped on the couch.

"Dude! Take off your shoes!" I exclaimed.

Steve jumped off the couch and stumbled into the coffee table.

Armi giggled. "Benny, you sound like Mom."

Mom called from the kitchen. "What's going on out there?"

"Nothing!" Armi yelled. This made us crack up.

It was easy to laugh now, knowing in a few hours Dad was going to walk through the door.

Armi fussed about the banner. "I still say it's too wrinkled."

Steve threw a cushion at her.

I reached up and smoothed out the biggest wrinkles. Armi smiled.

Steve said, "I better go. I don't wanna intrude on your family reunion."

I looked at the clock on the coffee table. "There's still time before Dad's transport arrives."

But even as Steve walked out the door, we saw Dad get out of a van.

"He's here!" Armi screeched so loud I thought I'd go deaf.

Mom ran out of the kitchen, drying her hands on a dish towel. As soon as she saw Dad, she burst into tears.

I nodded, unable to take my eyes off the soldier marching across the lawn. Was Dad really home?

Mom and Armi grabbed first hugs before Dad even made it to the door. I hung back, expecting him to smile or something. Instead, Dad shook his head and muttered, "I can't believe I'm finally here."

I touched Dad's arm and said, "I can't believe you're really here, either!"

Dad turned and looked at me. He didn't smile. He just stared and said, "You've grown a lot!"

Mom laughed and cried at the same time. "I told you! Benny's almost as big as you now."

As Dad stepped through the door, I expected to see his big, bright smile. Instead, his eyes just stared off into the distance. It was like he didn't recognize our living room. And I knew it couldn't be the new banner we'd put up.

"What's the matter?" Mom asked.

Dad studied the banner. Then he answered in a mumble. "Banners on the streets. Sometimes you slowed down to read them . . ." His voice trailed off. Mom put her arms around him and whispered in his ear.

Dad told Armida, "Thanks, *hija*! Your banner looks great."

But he kept looking around, like this was his first time in the house. What did he see? Somehow I knew it wasn't Armi and me and Mom in the lint-free living room.

CHAPTER 2

It didn't take long to realize that things weren't going to be the way they used to be. The first night he was home, Dad woke up screaming!

I thought the house was on fire. I jumped out of bed. Armi stood in the hall. She looked sleepy and puzzled.

We heard Mom say, "Wake up, Xavi!"

Finally, the terrible screaming stopped.

"It's just a dream," Mom said, trying to calm Dad down.

Armi and I looked at each other, wondering what to do. Should we knock on their door or just try to go back to sleep?

Mom opened the door. "It's okay," she said. "He just had a nightmare."

I looked past her and saw Dad sitting up in bed. He was covered in sweat. He saw me looking and managed a weak smile. "Sorry," he said. "Sorry to wake you both."

Mom went to the kitchen to get him a glass of water. It reminded me of when I used to have nightmares. I wanted to ask him what it was about. But the darkness and the distance in his eyes made me back off.

"It's okay, *hijos*," Dad said. "Go back to sleep."

So Armi and I shuffled back to bed. But it was hard to fall back to sleep with Dad's screams echoing in my ears.

I had hoped Dad would have some exciting war stories. I wanted tough stuff to tell my friends. But Dad came back from the war real quiet. He didn't sing, and he didn't talk much. He stared into space a lot. And he yelled.

17

"What is the garbage doing in the can?" he shouted one night.

I was supposed to put it out while Armi did the dishes. But Steve called. Besides, in Benito's *casa* nobody had cared when the garbage got bagged—as long as it was on the curb before the truck. I told Dad, "The truck doesn't come until tomorrow morning."

Dad's eyes darkened. "I don't want to hear any excuses. I told you to bag it after supper."

I shrugged and said, "Stop stressing." That's what Steve always told me.

Dad slammed the table so hard the sugar bowl rattled. "You'll bag it now!"

I was already bagging the garbage by the time he had stopped yelling.

"Chill out, see?" I said. "It's already done." I slung the bag over my shoulder like Santa Claus.

When I dumped it in the outside can I banged the lid a few times because I felt so mad. Why did Dad have to make such a big deal out of everything? It's like stressing was his new hobby.

Since the factory where he used to work closed, Dad had plenty of time to stress. We were surviving on Mom's salary, but I couldn't wait for him to get a new job. Dad being home all the time was driving us all crazy!

It was really hard being around him. It was like his eyes were marbles that rolled away from my gaze. Before Dad came home, I thought I was going to hear about battles and fighting. The first time I did, I felt like a fool for wanting to hear a war story.

One day before supper, I decided to lighten the mood. I took the soccer ball out of the closet and said, "Hey, Dad!"

I expected him to smile. And maybe say something like, "Great idea, let's play!"

Instead, his eyes got all huge. "Get that thing out of here!" he growled.

You would've thought I'd taken a rat out of the closet.

I tossed the ball in the closet and pulled the door shut. "It's gone," I assured him. Dad continued to stare at the spot where the ball had been.

I said, "It's just a ball."

Dad shook his head and began in a quiet voice, "Kids were playing soccer. The day Dave died, kids were out playing soccer."

Dave had been Dad's best friend in his unit. He had been in lots of the pictures Dad sent home. And then he wasn't. Maybe Dad had told Mom that Dave had died. But she didn't tell us. Mom never wanted Armi to worry. She's thirteen, but Mom still treats her like a baby.

Dad droned on. "The kids kicked their ball into the road. Our convoy stopped and then suddenly . . ."

I tried to meet his eyes, to make sure he was okay.

Dad pointed his finger at me like a gun. "POP! POP! POP!" he continued. "And Dave's brains were just a stain on my shirt—like a pink mist."

Dad looked down at his shoulder, as if the stain was still there. It was eerie.

CHAPTER 3

Even time changed after Dad got back from Iraq. Dad was so used to army time he didn't say five A.M. anymore. Now it was oh-five-hundred hours. And we had to be out of our racks—that's army talk for bed—by oh-five-hundred every morning, even on weekends!

Steve sympathized. "Doesn't your dad know it's Sunday?"

I shrugged. It was hard to know what my father was thinking. Every day blended into the one before. He didn't work, but he didn't relax, either.

We kept hoping things would get better. But they seemed to be getting worse!

When supper was ready, Dad didn't yell "suppertime" or "come and get it!" He shouted, "Eighteen hours!" And Armi and I had to report for mess call or there'd be no end to the yelling.

Like one afternoon, I was doing homework in my room. Dad called us to the table.

I yelled, "I'll be right there."

I figured they'd start eating without me. Instead, after a few minutes, I heard loud footsteps approaching my door.

Dad didn't just knock. He pounded so hard the door jumped on its hinges. "Everyone's waiting, Benito."

"I'll be right . . ."

The door flew open with such force it almost bounced closed again. He yelled in my face like a drill instructor, "Get to dinner now or you'll lose privileges!"

I was so mad, I thought I'd explode. What

right did he have to just walk into my room? He wasn't the only man in our house. I shouted back, "I'm not in your army!"

Dad fumed. His fists clenched. I could tell he wanted to hit me. I was almost daring him to, because I was so sick of his rules.

I felt embarrassed, because I knew the Joneses could hear all the shouting. You can't exactly share an attached house without hearing each other's noise.

Grown men aren't supposed to have screaming nightmares. But Dad had them at least once a week. He woke us all up, and the Joneses, too.

Steve complained, "The army hours are bad enough, but the shouting at night . . ."

I knew what he meant. Dad's screams infected me with a terrible fear.

Steve asked, "Can't you do something about your dad?"

I looked Steve in the eye and demanded, "Like what?"

Steve didn't know what to say. How can you tell a grown man what to do?

Sometimes dads just wig out. Steve's dad left years ago. That's why he and his brothers and sisters lived with their grandma. Steve seemed okay with it.

But I didn't want to lose my dad. I had always figured he was better than that. I had expected him to come home a hero. I think Dad had expected that, too. So this whole nightmares thing was a rude surprise.

Mom said, "This too shall pass." I was not sure what she meant by that. She told me and Armi to be patient with Dad. But I couldn't help feeling frustrated. He had been home for a few weeks. When would he start singing and cooking? When would things get back to normal?

CHAPTER 4

Weeks went by. I was tired of walking on my tiptoes. I missed kicking the ball around with my dad. But any time I thought about taking the ball out of the closet, I remembered Dad's story about the pink mist and the day Dave was killed.

I switched to practicing soccer in the gym or on the field after school. It was good for my game because it was better to practice with a bunch of players anyway.

And it was fun because the soccer squad was a great bunch of guys, like our captain, Rob. He's the kind of guy you want on your side. Rob always put in the extra effort. And that made everyone want to do their best.

Coach Wunderman gave us pointers, too. He was okay for a teacher. He loved soccer, and he really knew the moves. He was strict, but his rules were for the good of the team.

I used to feel that way about Dad. He was the wise and good captain of our family team. But now I just wanted to get away from him and his crazy rages.

So I spent all my spare time with the squad. One day, at the end of practice, Coach Wunderman said, "Hey, Benito, how about helping to sell tickets for the Bowling Night fund-raiser? We need to get sponsors, too."

I'm not usually the clipboard-and-cause type. But I was game for anything that kept me out of the house. So I started spending most of my time after school selling fund-raiser tickets.

One night at supper, Mom gushed, "I'm glad you're showing some school spirit."

I didn't have the heart to tell her I just wanted to stay away from Dad.

On the afternoon of the Friday-night fund-raiser, Coach Wunderman announced that I had sold more tickets than anyone else in the squad. He said, "Three cheers for Benito! He's our new sales-and-sponsorship captain!"

It took me by surprise. Did I sign up for that? I didn't know how to say no to the coach or my cheering teammates. Besides, if I had sold the most tickets, maybe I was the right guy for the job.

Now the only problem about the fund-raiser was Dad. I had bought four tickets for us, assuming he would come. Now I wasn't so sure that I wanted him to.

After school, I hid out at Steve's. We were supposed to be doing our homework. But I couldn't concentrate.

"I'm dreading the fund-raiser," I said.

Steve looked up from his math, surprised. "You kidding? I thought you loved bowling."

"I do, but my dad . . ."

Steve knew what I was talking about. After all, he heard the screams at night. But he said, "Chill out. Your dad will be okay. It's just bowling. It's not like it's paintball—or soccer."

I hated that Steve knew how crazy Dad had been acting. But I guessed that having a dad who freaks out over a soccer ball was better than having no dad at all. At least that's what I told myself.

But I still couldn't focus on my homework. Something was eating at me. And I just had to say it out loud before I busted. "Sometimes I wish . . ."

Steve put his pencil in his math book to mark the page. He looked up at me, waiting for me to finish the sentence. But now that I had his attention, I couldn't quite bring myself to say it. Steve said, "Yeah, you wish . . . what?"

"Dad had never come home." When I said the words, they sounded even more horrible than they did in my head!

"I know what you mean," Steve said. "I sometimes think about my dad coming back. But a lot of times I'm glad he's gone."

There was an awkward silence. Neither one of us wanted to get back to our homework, so I asked, "Is your grandma coming to the fund-raiser?"

Steve nodded. "You know she'd never pass up a chance for gossip and bowling."

We did a little more homework before it was time for me to go home. At dinner, I tried to tell myself Steve was right. Dad would be okay at the fund-raiser.

CHAPTER 5

As soon as we arrived at the bowling alley, it seemed like Dad went to his dark place. He went on and on about how he had to pay "good money" for the *zapatos feos*. Then he put the "stinking things" on his feet.

Mom sighed.

Dad stared down at his feet, and he winced at the loud music.

Mom patted his hand soothingly. But Dad continued to frown. He looked around nervously and said, "I didn't realize it would be so crowded."

Mom said, "That's because our son did such a good job selling tickets!" Her cheerful voice sounded forced.

The bowling alley got even more crowded. Some of the other soccer mothers waved to Mom. She waved back but didn't let go of Dad's hand.

Mom said, "Come on. Let's go say hello to everyone."

Dad shook his head. "You go ahead. I'll be fine here."

Mom hesitated.

Dad let go of her hand. Then he said, "Go on."

The other mothers were all laughing and talking. Mom walked over to them, and the talking and laughing got even louder.

Dad paced nervously. He said, "Maybe I should step outside for a while."

"You can't go outside in bowling shoes," Armi reminded him.

I tried to catch his eye. But Dad wouldn't return my gaze.

I rushed over to Mom. I didn't want to say anything in front of the other mothers, but I didn't have to. Mom took one look at Dad and knew something was very wrong.

She rushed back to him. But it was too late! Dad suddenly kicked off the stupid shoes. He stood there in his socks and began to rant, "Camel spiders! They get in your boots at night. They get as big as your fist!"

Mom tugged his arm and whispered in his ear. "There are no camel spiders in Texas."

She held the bowling shoes out to him. But Dad slapped them out of her hands. They clattered to the wooden floor.

By now everyone was staring at my crazy father. All the chatter and laughter was silent. There was just loud music and embarrassment.

I looked around at all the staring eyes. I couldn't stand it anymore. I ran for the nearest exit. But Mr. Mason, the manager, yelled after me, "You can't leave in those shoes!"

I tore off the stupid shoes and hurled them. I almost threw them through the window! But the shoes just hit the wooden frame.

"You're lucky you didn't break the glass, kid!" Mr. Mason exclaimed. He was fuming about me and my crazy dad making a scene.

Then Coach Wunderman ran up. He put his arm around Mr. Mason's shoulders and walked him back into the building. By now, Mom, Dad, and Armi were outside. They had brought my regular shoes. We all went home.

Later that night, I couldn't stand being in the house with Dad. So I snuck over to Steve's. He told me, "Chill out! It's not the end of the world. You weren't thrown in jail or kicked off the soccer squad."

"Nah, just humiliated in front of half the school," I snapped. I thought my best friend would understand.

Steve laughed and said, "You didn't sell that many tickets."

"Okay, a quarter of the school," I said. "But still, you know they'll all be gossiping about it, and their families will, too. I'll be the talk of the school, like Amber."

Everyone at Southside High had talked about Amber. Last year she had gotten so drunk at this big party that she had died of alcohol poisoning. I used to think that you'd puke your guts out long before you would die. But apparently Amber passed out and never woke up. It was gossip for weeks.

I couldn't stand the thought of being the latest pity story to buzz around the halls and cafeteria. I wanted to go somewhere else—but where?

The digital clock behind Steve's head blinked angry red numbers at me. I said, "I better get going. I'm out past 'curfew.'"

Steve said, "I'll see you tomorrow after chores." Then he quoted Grandma Jones, saying "Everything will look better in the morning."

She always said that. But was it really true?

CHAPTER 6

The next morning was pretty miserable for me. For Dad, Saturday was inspection day.

Armi and I scrambled to get our rooms clean so we could start enjoying the weekend. I stuffed everything into my closet. Then I sprayed furniture polish on a rag and dragged it over the dustiest places.

The lemon smell was usually enough to satisfy Mom. But Dad could find dust in places I barely knew existed.

I looked at the clock. It was already after ten. Steve would be done with his chores.

Then I heard Dad thunder, "When was the last time you rotated this rack?"

The door to Armi's room was open.

"Rotate my bed? What are you talking about?" she asked.

Mom stopped vacuuming long enough to explain, "He means flip the mattress. It'll wear out more evenly."

Armi whined, "Why didn't you tell me that before I changed my sheets?"

Dad gritted his teeth. "Just do it!" Then he saw me in the doorway and shouted, "You too!"

Mom whispered, "Please, *hijos*. Don't push him today." Then she turned the vacuum cleaner back on and hummed back into the living room.

So Armi and I took the clean sheets off our beds. We flipped our mattresses and put the sheets back on. Then we submitted to a second inspection.

While Dad bounced a quarter off Armi's

blanket, I actually folded all the clothes stuffed in the bottom of my closet. I didn't want to deal with Dad if he found them.

When he looked at the tidy closet floor, Dad nodded. Then he surprised me by saying, "I'm sorry about my . . . outburst last night at the bowling alley."

His eyes quickly shifted from mine to the freshly vacuumed floor. He wiped tears from the corners of his eyes.

I didn't know what to say. Dad said he was sorry, so I was supposed to forgive him. But that weepy apology was even worse than the camel-spider rant. Dads weren't supposed to cry! I felt like I had to get out.

I ran over to Steve's house. As usual, he said, "Chill out, dude! Why are you always stressing?"

I couldn't bear to tell him about Dad's tearful apology. It was bad enough that a quarter of the school already knew about his bowling alley behavior.

Again, I wondered what it would have been like if Dad hadn't come home. I imagined

Mom as the dignified widow. Armi as the brave daughter. And I would be the man of the house. Despite my tragic loss, I would have still sold more fund-raiser tickets than anyone on the squad. I would be a hero.

But there was nothing heroic about being the son of someone crazy. In fact, it was kind of the opposite.

My dad had freaked out about imaginary spiders in front of just about everyone I knew! And Steve had just told me to chill out.

Steve and I went over to his cousin Ernie's apartment building to round up some guys to play basketball at the park. I didn't want to think. I just dribbled and shot.

Some of the guys on the court started to tease me about the bowling alley incident. Ernie started it. "Hey, Benny! Just pretend the basket's the bowling-alley window."

I dribbled right past Ernie as if he didn't exist. Others laughed, so Ernie kept at it. "Or you can pretend there's a spider under the basket and the only way to smoosh it is . . ."

Steve blocked Ernie hard with his

muscular shoulder. Ernie had to shuffle fast to stay on his feet. "Shut up, Evie!" Steve said.

Ernie fumed. He hated being called by a girl's name. Ernie was taller than Steve but not nearly as strong. Nobody wanted to mess with Steve. So finally, they just shut up and played.

I was grateful, but it made me feel like a girl who needed her boyfriend to defend her. I tried to concentrate on the game. But I couldn't help worrying that this was only the beginning of the teasing. What would happen at school on Monday?

CHAPTER 7

In Casa Benito, Sunday morning meant sleeping late and eating waffles in our jammies. But once Dad came home, Platoon Rodriguez woke up at the crack of crazy.

The Sunday after the fund-raiser, Mom cooked oatmeal because that's what Commander Dad wanted. Believe me, when you're used to waffles, oatmeal just doesn't cut it.

"Let's go to church this morning!" Mom suggested with forced cheer.

We usually only went on holidays or for weddings and stuff. But I guess she thought church would make us feel better.

Armi groaned. "Please don't make me dress up."

"When I was your age, little girls loved to dress up," Mom said for the three-millionth time.

Armi stomped up the stairs, muttering, "I'm not a little girl!"

But she put on one of her church dresses anyway.

Dad looked at me and said, "Dress up. You too."

I rolled my eyes.

Dad's eyebrows lifted as his stare deepened. I didn't move a muscle, just stared right back into the black pits of his angry eyes. I knew I should move. I knew dressing up for church was no big deal. But somehow I just couldn't stand knuckling under to him. I didn't blink, and neither did Dad.

SNAP! Mom snapped her fingers and broke the tension. "It's not a staring contest.

It's Sunday. Now go get your church clothes on—both of you!"

We laughed, but the tension crept back in during the short walk around the block to the church. The morning was still new, but the Texas sun already scorched us during our stroll.

Dad didn't walk like Dad any more. He walked stiffly, like a soldier. Armi had to trot to keep up.

When we got to church, Armi let out a loud sigh as she pulled the dress away from her body. She whined, "I hate this dress."

Mom looked like she wanted to yell, but we were in church. So she took a deep breath. "Let's all try to be grateful for what we have."

I looked at Dad. He was standing "at ease," but he didn't look at ease at all. He looked like he was seeing camel spiders everywhere.

Mom guided him down the aisle toward an empty pew. I thought people were staring at us because we weren't Sunday regulars.

Dad gripped the hymn book tightly. Mom covered his shaking hand with hers. But every other part of him twitched with restless movements. His legs vibrated to an unheard drum. His haunted eyes darted over the crowded pews.

I could feel the strange intensity of my father's gaze.

He focused on the hymn book in his hands. But his knees kept jumping.

Mom asked, "Do you need to take a walk outside?"

Dad shook his head, like a kid resolving not to puke in the car. Like he was telling himself he could stand it. He would be okay.

He took a deep breath. But my breaths were shallow. I wished Mom would offer me a walk outside. I wished I had the guts to run out of the church and breathe!

Instead, I listened politely as the service began. I wanted to feel comforted by the priest's words, but I found myself looking around the church with Dad's eyes. I saw a bomb in every satchel, a potential insurgent sitting in every pew.

Not even the hymns could lift my heavy heart. I was too aware of the silence surrounding Dad. He wasn't singing, and I started to wonder if he even could.

My legs were almost as jumpy as Dad's. They wanted to be kicking a soccer ball. I could practically hear the satisfying *THWACK* sound—like when my foot smacked the ball just right. But now I couldn't even practice soccer after church unless I went to the park, out of Dad's sight.

Mass felt like it lasted forever! Afterward, Dad took us out for lunch. It was supposed to be a treat. But I just wanted the day to be over. Except I was also dreading Monday. I just wanted to get out of my own skin.

CHAPTER 8

S top stressing," Steve said. "Everyone will forget about you over the weekend. You're not the center of the universe, you know."

Steve was right about the universe but wrong about the gossips at Southside. By Monday, the stars and planets had done their usual thing. But everyone from Southside was still buzzing about me and Dad acting like crazies at the bowling alley Friday night.

The lies grew like weeds until Dad had practically killed a waitress and I had broken every window in the place. Worst of all, I had a new nickname: Camel Spider.

As I boarded the bus, I heard giggles and whispers.

Steve scowled and the kids nearest us shut up.

But once Steve and I settled down, I heard, "Hey, Camel Spider!"

"Look what just crawled out of someone's shoe!"

"Let's squish it."

I couldn't even walk down a hall without someone singing the Spider-Man theme song or "The Itsy-Bitsy Spider."

In homeroom, when the teacher called my name, someone whispered "Camel Spider" at the same time. I turned around to see who'd done it. But everyone just stared at me. And some of them laughed.

Lunch was even worse. Just as I walked past the table where the football team sat, one of them screamed, "Look out! Camel Spider!"

The rest of the team laughed.

Then I heard Paige, the head cheerleader, say, "Stop it! It isn't Benny's fault his father's crazy."

I'm not sure what felt worse, the laughter or the pity. Even kids I had thought were my friends joined in on the teasing.

Before phys ed, Coach Wunderman pulled me aside and advised, "Just ignore them."

That was easy for him to say. Part of me thought they were right. I mean, they were teasing me because they thought my dad was crazy. Well, maybe he was. What was I supposed to do about it?

Coach said, "Focus on the future."

I thought he was talking about college and all that. But then he added, "Squad Night is coming up this weekend."

My stomach flip-flopped. Just what I needed: another chance for my father to freak out in front of everyone! Squad Night was a really big deal at Southside. Every year, every team had a chance to beat the football team at their own game. The basketball team played a half-court game against the football team. Us soccer guys tried to prove that footballers aren't the only ones who can kick a ball.

Sure, it wasn't exactly fair. I mean the swim team certainly knows more about the butterfly stroke than the football team. But it kind of makes up for every other day of the year, when the football team acts like it owns the whole school.

Last year, the soccer squad creamed the football team. And I had done my part. But with everything that had been going on . . .

Coach clapped me on the back. "The way you've been training lately, you're sure to score a bunch of points for the squad." I nodded. But I was having a lot of trouble caring about helping the soccer squad beat the football team. All I wanted to do was hide under a rock. Be someplace dark, where no one could see me. I realized I was thinking like a camel spider!

Coach Wunderman blew his whistle for the soccer game to begin. I forced myself to pay attention. As if it would really make any difference. Dad would still be crazy when he came to Squad Night, whether we won this game or not. But I ran fast, as if I could outrun shame.

Coach yelled out, "Benito's free!"

The squad captain, Rob, passed the ball to me. Without thinking, I kicked it past the opposition's goalie. We won!

For a wonderful moment, that's all that mattered. I scored the winning goal! Then reality rushed back, like a hard pass hitting me in the stomach. What was going to happen at Squad Night? How would Dad act? Would he go crazy from the noise and attention? Would I?

Everyone clapped me on the back. I wanted to share their good cheer. Yet I was frowning. I was staring down at my sneakers, but I was seeing bowling shoes. I kept picturing those *zapatos feos* flying through the air toward the alley window.

Rob patted me on the shoulder. He grinned and said, "You really can kick like Spider Man."

I knew he was only teasing. But it drove me nuts anyway.

CHAPTER 9

For the rest of the school day, my thoughts kept churning. What if Squad Night was an even bigger disaster than the bowling fund-raiser?

English class burbled in the background, like the dim soundtrack to the miserable movie in my mind. I knew I should be paying attention but . . .

"Benito? I asked you a question." Mrs. McCormack's voice cut through my web of worries.

I looked up and realized the whole class was staring at me. Our teacher expected an answer, and I didn't even know the question!

Mrs. McCormack prompted me, "I asked you about the story on page 42."

I fumbled with my books. I wasn't even sure which book she was talking about! Everyone laughed. Then the bell rang.

Mrs. McCormack said, "Benito, please stay for a few minutes."

The other students rushed past me while I sat in my chair feeling like an idiot. I expected the teacher to yell at me. Instead, she waited for the last stragglers to leave. Then Mrs. McCormack asked, "Benito, what's wrong?"

I didn't know how to answer. I could have said, "My dad came home crazy." But that would make it seem like I was tattling on my old man.

And it wasn't like he had signed up for crazy. Dad had signed up to be a hero. The crazy part just sort of happened.

I mean, wouldn't you think you'd come home from the army braver and stronger than you went in? Who would have guessed that

Dad would come home so . . . scared?

Mrs. McCormack cleared her throat. "Lately you seem distracted . . ."

The silence grew. I knew this was the part where I was supposed to say something. But what could I say?

Mrs. McCormack reached into her desk and handed me a small notebook. "Here. Write a journal. Express yourself. Whatever's wrong, it will make you feel better."

I almost laughed out loud. But I stopped myself just in time. I didn't want to be rude. She didn't mean to be ridiculous.

As teachers went, Mrs. McC was all right. But as for scribbling in a diary . . . That was strictly for gooey schoolgirls and aspiring assassins. Armi might want to gush about her latest crush, but I . . .

I tucked the notebook in my backpack and said, "Thank you."

Mrs. McC looked me right in the eyes and replied, "Trust me." Then she added, "Just write."

CHAPTER 10

I zipped my backpack shut and slung it over my shoulder. Then I hurried to the gym to get ready for soccer practice. The halls were mostly deserted. My footsteps echoed like lonely drums.

Coach Wunderman and the rest of the squad were already out on the field. I ran to meet them.

I only half-listened to Coach's pep talk. I just wanted to run under the open sky. I wanted to feel fast!

One of our center forwards was sick.
So coach gave me a chance to show what I
could do.

As soon as the scrimmage began, I forgot
all about Dad. It felt great to be thinking
about nothing except moving the ball down
the field.

I knew Coach wouldn't like it if I hogged
the ball. So I passed it to Rob. Then I raced
ahead and Rob passed it back to me. Pretty
soon I was close enough to the goal to make
the shot. But Jake was closer, and no one was
guarding him. So I passed it to him, and we
scored!

It was a real pretty thing. Coach blew
his whistle and shouted, "That's the kind of
teamwork I'm talking about!"

The rest of practice went even better. I
made several more great passes and scored on
my own, too. Coach clapped me on the back
and said, "Keep practicing the way you have
been, and you'll play center yet!"

For the first time since Dad had come
home, I felt really good!

Just before our usual quitting time, Coach Wunderman announced, "I have something to share with all of you."

He pulled out a big envelope. "It's from Dustin."

Some of the new players didn't know our former teammate. Dustin had moved to Dallas after our sophomore year.

He used to live on my block, so we used to hang out all the time. But talking on the phone isn't the same as kicking a soccer ball together. So we'd mostly lost touch.

Coach opened the envelope and took out a bunch of newspaper pages. Each page had a yellow sticky-note on it.

Coach passed out the pages by name. Rob got his first. Then Coach called, "Benny!"

Everyone was already reading Rob's newspaper. He held it over his head so we could all see the full-color picture of Dustin kicking a soccer ball right over the goalie's shoulder toward the net.

Rob said, "The caption reads, 'Dustin Charles scores the winning goal for South Dallas High School.'"

I read the yellow sticky stuck to my copy of the front page. It said, "Benny, Dallas is great! You should visit. Wish you were on my team here!" Then he signed, in big, bold letters, Dusty C., just like he was already a famous athlete.

It felt good to know Dustin wished I was on his team. Then I had a thought: *What if I was? What if I went to Dallas?*

I could leave all my camel-spider problems and my crazy dad behind. Dustin and I could work up some killer moves. We'd become star soccer players!

Maybe this was the answer to my problems with my dad.

ChAPTER 11

My fingers shook as I scrambled to get
dressed in the locker room. It was almost
like my worries had washed off with the sweat.
The answer seemed so easy: just pack a bag
and go live with Dusty.

I imagined a newspaper clipping showing
me and Dustin scoring the winning goal for
the South Dallas High team.

It would be strange to wear different
colors, to play for a different school. But at

least nobody in Dallas knew about the camel-spider incident!

I could start fresh. I could have a whole new attitude. Maybe I'd be cool like Steve, instead of always stressing. Dusty was cool. Maybe I could learn to be.

I wondered if I should change my name when I got there. Dusty probably wouldn't rat me out. He liked spies and stuff. I could be whoever I wanted to be!

I almost missed my bus stop, dreaming about my brand-new life.

When I got home, I was hoping to avoid Dad. I was in luck. Armi was home alone. She said, "Mom and Dad are at the V.A. hospital."

I shuddered. I'd never been to a Veteran's Administration hospital. But I'd seen some in movies. You always saw guys in wheelchairs and guys with stumps instead of limbs who were freaked out because they came home broken.

Armi rattled on. "Mom called. The doctors say Dad has PTSD, or something like that."

I knew what those initials stood for. "Post-Traumatic Stress Disorder," I said.

"Yeah, that's it. And they're going to give him medicine and therapy," Armi said. "Mom says things are gonna get better."

I wanted to believe that. I didn't want to run away. But would Dad be better in time for Squad Night?

I imagined walking down school halls hearing "Camel Spider" for months, and I realized this was the perfect time to pack and get out. "Yeah, whatever," I said. "I'll see you at dinner."

I bounded upstairs before Armi could ask any nosy little-sister questions.

I was cramming my favorite stuff in a duffle bag when Armi opened the door. She asked, "Where are you going?"

"Don't you ever knock?" I shouted. But I wasn't really angry with Armi. I was angry with myself for forgetting to lock the door.

Armi stared at the duffle, growing more suspicious by the second. So I quickly fibbed, "I'm staying over at Steve's."

My sister was skeptical. "You never pack this much just to go next door. You just run back and forth all night."

Before I could think of another lie, she went on, "Besides, Steve's grandma doesn't allow sleepovers on school nights."

"Okay, Sherlock. I'm getting out of here. But if you tell, I'll never speak to you again."

It was hard to imagine never talking to Armi anymore. But the threat scared her.

"You can't run away!" she yelled.

That made me all the more determined. Why couldn't I go somewhere else?

"What about school?" Armi asked. "You can't just leave!"

Her words were just noise. My mind was miles ahead, at the bus station, buying a ticket for Dallas.

"I can't tell you where I'm going," I said. "Tell Mom and Dad not to worry. I just need some space. I'll call when I get settled."

Armi looked scared. I wanted to hug her. But if I did, I knew I would chicken out.

I didn't want to chicken out. I had to go! I needed to start a new life in Dallas.

CHAPTER 12

I had never realized how far away the bus station was. There was a bus stop nearby, but I didn't want to stand there waiting and have someone see me. So I was all sweaty by the time I got to the main road.

My duffle bag got heavier with each step. Cars whizzed past. I envied their speed. It would be so easy to jump in someone's air-conditioned car.

I knew hitchhiking was dangerous. But then I thought, *How bad could it be with all this traffic?* I decided to be careful. I would take a really good look at the driver before I got in the car.

I turned around and stuck out my thumb. Cars kept whizzing by. They didn't even slow down.

What if no one picked me up? Would I wind up walking backward all the way to the station?

I looked over my shoulder and tried to do one of those long math problems in my head. If the average speed limit on the road to the station is thirty-five miles per hour, and the trip takes . . .

A car slowed down! I tried to peer through the window, but all I saw was glare.

The passenger door opened. "Hop in!" a man's voice said. "Air-conditioning's getting out, and I finally got it cool in here."

I leaned my head in and saw a clean-cut, middle-aged man. He didn't seem too big and muscle-bound or especially mean. I didn't see a shotgun on the dashboard or any beers on the floorboards.

I got in and closed the door behind me. The cool air felt great!

The car pulled away. "How long have you been walking?" the man asked.

I looked at the dashboard clock. Then I looked at my watch. Had it only been an hour and a half since I left home?

The man asked, "How far are you going?"

"I'm visiting a friend in . . ." saying "Dallas" probably wouldn't matter. But I didn't want to say too much. So I let the sentence trail off. I began again. "I'm visiting a friend. He's sick. Or I wouldn't be traveling on a school night."

"I hope you don't have to travel too far all alone," the man said.

His eyes searched my face as I sank into the seat. "I worry about a good-looking kid like you, traveling all alone."

Something just didn't feel right, and I immediately regretted getting in. I wondered if I should brag about knowing karate. Or maybe just play it cool 'til the car stopped at a light and then jump out?

My eyes darted to the car door. Was it locked? Could I just flip it open?

There was no time to plan. I had to act. The green light up ahead turned amber. The car would have to stop or run a red. And that might draw cops.

The car slowed. The man glanced away from the road. I pretended I was just listening to the radio. I even tapped my fingers in time to the music.

His eyes drifted back to the road. I lifted the lever, opened the door, and jumped out.

I was way up the street before the driver had time to react. But just in case, I turned off the main street and ran along the parallel road. I risked a look over my shoulder but didn't see the car.

I ran past puzzled pedestrians, past old people with packages and young moms with baby carriages. I was so scared, I barely felt the weight of the heavy duffle bag.

It wasn't as heavy as the "ruck" Dad had carried with all his equipment. But it got awfully heavy once the panic left me. Still, I didn't slow down.

CHAPTER 13

S weat poured down my face, but I kept
running. Finally, I saw the bus station. The
relief gave my legs new strength. The station
would be nice and air-conditioned, and soon
I would be buying a ticket to Dallas! I could
catch my breath, get a drink of water, and be
on my way to a new life.

I had no idea what a ticket to Dallas
would cost. I wondered if the ticket seller
would ask my name. I tried to remember my

last bus trip. We had all gone to say good-bye to Dad. But Mom had bought those tickets.

I decided if the ticket seller asked, I would be Nate Austin. Having an alias made me feel like a spy.

The smell of hot dogs floated on the building's cool air. I was so hungry! But I didn't want to spend money on food until I bought the ticket. One way. That was something new. I had never gone anywhere one-way before.

I steadied my voice as I stood before the ticket window. "One-way to Dallas, please."

The ticket took almost all the cash I had! Mowing lawns doesn't add up to much—especially if you like to buy video games. I've never been much of a saver. I guessed I wouldn't be buying any hot dogs. But at least I would soon be on my way.

He handed me the ticket. "Next bus leaves at 10:15."

I couldn't believe my ears. It was only seven P.M. I had a long wait.

"Gate 3, 10:15," the seller said. Then he added, "Next!"

The person behind me moved up to the counter. I stepped away, clinging to the ticket in one hand and holding my change in the other. It was going to be a long, hungry few hours!

I looked for a water fountain. At least that was free. As I bent to drink the cool water, I noticed a bum in an army surplus jacket picking food out of a garbage can. He fished out a half-eaten sandwich and put it in one of the big pockets of his old fatigue jacket.

It was really weird, but I was jealous of a bum because he had half a sandwich and I didn't. And he was used to Dumpster diving. I was used to home-cooked meals on clean plates.

I couldn't believe what I was thinking. But as I walked past the garbage can, this guy in a suit tossed in a barely eaten hot dog. I grabbed it and wolfed it down. The bum glared at me. I looked away.

It wasn't my fault he had no money. I hardly had any money, either. And if I spent it all now, I wouldn't have any for the trip.

But the man's angry glare haunted me, especially because of his army jacket. Had he really been a soldier? Then, once again, I thought about my dad.

CHAPTER 14

A rmi's words echoed in my mind. "Dad has PTSD." But I wondered: What does that really mean?

Mrs. McCormack's favorite phrase popped into my head. "Look it up!" I noticed a for-pay computer terminal near the bus station's pay phones and vending machines. I figured it would be a good place to kill time before the bus left, even if it took some of my remaining change.

After logging onto the station's public computer, I started searching for the info I wanted: articles and web pages about soldiers, trauma, and veterans.

I skimmed lots of articles, looking for an explanation. PTSD is a mental and emotional war wound, an illness, a syndrome.

I usually skipped to the parts that described the symptoms: nightmares, sleeplessness, tension, mood swings, rage, fear of crowds, loss of joy, and a change in habits. Dad had a classic case.

This made me feel both better and worse. I had a name for his problem, but what about the cure?

I clicked on more links. They all talked about therapy and pills. These would help. But there was no quick fix.

Suddenly, I felt tired. I didn't want to feel sorry for my father. I just wanted to get away from the crazy and feel okay again. I wanted to be Benito, not Camel Spider. And if I couldn't be Benito, I'd become Nate Austin. That was a cool name.

Nate Austin lived in Dallas. His dad wasn't crazy. Nate Austin was just fine.

I thought about Dusty's loud laugh and his smooth soccer moves. We would have tons of practice time if I was staying at his house. It would be great to have some fun and forget about camel spiders and bowling shoes.

My stomach growled. That hot dog hadn't been a lot to go on. I hoped Dustin's mom was a good cook. I remembered him bringing great cupcakes for a bake sale one time. But I didn't know if they had been homemade or store-bought.

I looked at my watch. My folks would be done with supper. I bet they had something good. My stomach growled louder. Anything would have been good right then.

Chapter 15

There was still lots of time before the bus left. But I had read all I could about PTSD. My brain was spinning.

I opened my duffle bag. I thought I could turn off the sound on my video game and play for a while. I hadn't packed any books, because I had figured I'd start school fresh in Dallas. But I had packed the little notebook Mrs. McCormack had given me. I could still hear her urging me, "Just write."

I thought I'd be writing about soccer victories with Dusty. But those hadn't happened yet.

I took out the notebook and a pen. Blank pages beckoned in Mrs. McC's voice, "Just write. It will make you feel better. I promise."

I was skeptical. How could writing make someone feel better? But the teacher had seemed so positive.

I decided to give it a try. At first I didn't know what to say. How could I pick just one thought out of the whole jumble in my head?

Then I figured it didn't really matter. I decided, just pick the first thought that comes into your brain.

While I was writing that, the next one bumped into it. And pretty soon all the thoughts were bumping into each other, like crowds waiting for a turn on a carnival ride.

My hands couldn't keep up with my brain. All the thoughts wanted their turn on the page. Lines turned into paragraphs, paragraphs into pages. My handwriting got sloppier and sloppier. But I felt better!

It was like the crowd in my head had gone home. I looked down at the scribbled pages and yawned.

I put my head on my hands to rest my eyes. I didn't even realize I'd fallen asleep until the noise of passengers getting on a 9:30 bus to somewhere else woke me up. *I have got to get moving*, I thought.

CHAPTER 16

The hands on the bus station clock slowly crawled toward 10:15. Finally, I heard "all passengers bound for Dallas," and I boarded the bus. It wasn't crowded, so I got two whole seats to myself.

I felt a rush of excitement as the bus pulled out of the station. I was on my way! I wanted to hang onto that feeling. But worries crept into the flow of my thoughts. What if I couldn't keep Dustin's parents from calling mine? How long would they let me stay? How much money would I need for an apartment? Would I even be able to get a job in Dallas? After all, I'd never had a job. I was a minor. I didn't have working papers.

The worries started piling up. What kind of a job would I be able to get if I didn't graduate from high school? Or was there some way I could graduate in Dallas without getting permission from my parents?

The bus slowed down. I looked at my watch. Dallas was at least a five-hour bus ride from Houston.

The loudspeaker crackled, and the driver announced, "We'll be taking a fifteen-minute break. There are refreshments and restrooms in the station. Be back on time!"

Refreshments and a bathroom that wasn't in a moving vehicle appealed to me. So did the chance to stretch my cramped legs.

I saw other passengers leaving their luggage. So I left my duffle bag on the seat. I figured nobody wanted my clothes and video game. At least I hoped not!

Besides, I wouldn't be gone long. I walked out to use the bathroom, past the closed ticket office. On the way back from the men's room, I saw a candy machine. I decided to spend my last few coins on a snack. I didn't want to be starving when the bus got to Dallas.

I studied all the choices: caramel, peanuts, almonds, chocolate. What I really wanted was a big plate of Dad's enchiladas.

I suddenly realized that someone was standing behind me—too close. I smelled stale cigarette smoke. Did someone else want to use the snack machine?

Before I had time to turn around, a gruff voice commanded, "Give me your money. Don't scream!"

My first instinct was to turn around. But something prodded me in the back. The gruff voice said, "You don't want to see my face—or I'll shoot!"

I reached into my pocket and dug out my wallet. I didn't even think about trying to take anything from it. I just handed it over.

My fingers were shaking. The thief's hands were quick and rough. He grabbed the wallet and said, "Good boy. Now say night-night."

I blinked. Did this creep just say "ni . . ."

At the edge of my vision, I saw a blur. Pain blasted the back of my head. I barely had time to think *Ow!* before the floor rushed up to meet me.

CHAPTER 17

I woke up in an ambulance. I heard the EMTs talking before they realized I was awake.

"His vitals are stabilizing," reported the one listening to my chest. He was a big man with short, red hair.

Cool hands adjusted the bandage around my head. The gauze muffled my hearing. "The bleeding has slowed. He may not even need stitches."

Each moment brought greater awareness. The ambulance siren screamed. Its wheels bounced over a pothole. My head hurt!

"His eyes are open," said the red-haired EMT.

His partner, a black woman, shined a light in my eyes. I wanted to cover them with my hands, but my arms were strapped down.

"How do you feel?" she asked.

I wanted to answer, "I'm all right. Just let me out of here." But my tongue felt all thick and clumsy. Finally I managed to mutter, "Okay."

"You took quite a blow to the head," the redhead said.

No kidding, I thought. But my slow tongue replied, "Yeah."

I wanted to ask a million questions: Am I paralyzed or just strapped down? Did the cops catch the creep who robbed me?

I saw my duffle bag at the foot of my stretcher. I wondered how it had gotten there—and how had I?

The woman patted my hand. "You'll be all right. When you didn't return to your seat, the bus driver went looking for you. When he found you, he called the police. They found your empty wallet and called your parents. They're already on their way to the hospital."

My stomach churned with fear. If Dad got angry about curfew or the garbage, how would he react to me running away and getting mugged?

The EMT studied my face and then asked, "What's the matter?"

I moaned, "My dad's going to kill me!"

She smiled and shook her head. "Your dad is going to be glad to see you in one piece."

I tried to turn away from her so she wouldn't see me cry. But moving my head hurt too much and made me dizzy.

"Just take it easy," the redhead said. "We're almost there."

I heard other sirens as the ambulance turned, slowed down, and then stopped.

I got dizzy all over again as the EMTs lowered the gurney onto the curb. I didn't want to puke, so I closed my eyes as they wheeled me into the hospital. The hallways stank of bleach.

A balding doctor examined me. I felt numb and far away.

"You're a lucky young man. You won't need stitches," the doctor said. "So we won't have to shave that thick hair of yours." He winked, and I tried to smile.

A nurse came up and told him that the police were waiting to take my statement. "Is he ready to talk, or should I tell them to come back later?"

The balding doctor took my pulse and looked into my eyes. "Are you ready to tell the officers what happened?"

My tongue didn't feel so thick anymore. "Sure, I guess so," I said.

The doctor smiled. He turned to the nurse. "Send them in, but don't let them stay long." Then he hurried off down the hall.

Two cops took my statement. They were really nice.

I had never been mugged before. I never thought something like that could happen to me—just to other people, you know, on TV.

The older officer asked most of the questions. The younger one just nodded and wrote down my answers.

Since I didn't know much, it didn't take very long. The young cop closed his notebook.

"Do you think you'll catch him?" I asked.

His partner shrugged and said, "I wouldn't count on recovering your cash. But we will certainly call you if we make an arrest. And please call us if you think of any other information that might help in our investigation."

On the way out, his young partner said, "You did the right thing. If you had resisted, it might have gone badly for you."

I shuddered at the close call. What if I had died? What if I had just hit the floor and never woke up—like poor Amber?

Running away had seemed like a good idea, but the thought of never seeing my family again, even my dad, was too much!

Still, I couldn't help wishing I'd done something all brave and Bruce Lee. I imagined myself stomping on the creep's foot and then shoving my elbow in his ribs. Then I would have turned around and grabbed his gun!

Of course, if the gun had gone off . . .

I fell asleep imagining the creep in handcuffs and the cops clapping me on the back, calling me a hero.

I woke up to the sound of Mom's voice. "*Mijo!* We were so worried!"

She and Dad stood in the doorway of my hospital room.

"Benny!" Dad said. There were tears in his eyes.

I wanted to be cool and grown-up, but I started crying, too.

CHAPTER 18

My wound wasn't serious, but I did have a concussion. The doctor let me go home that night with Mom and Dad. Mom wanted to take a few days off work to take care of me, but Dad said, "I'm not working. I can take care of Benny." Then he smiled. It wasn't the big, bright grin of Dad before Iraq. But it was a start.

And I didn't exactly object to staying home from school. I wanted the kids at Southside to have time to forget about calling me Camel Spider.

Steve stopped by after school every day. He brought my homework. He also told me, "No one's talking about the camel spider thing anymore. The big rumor is that some of the football players might be on steroids! Coach Green is furious. Because if it's true, the guys won't be able to compete on Squad Night."

I wasn't mean enough to be happy about news like that. But I couldn't help being glad that I was no longer the hot gossip of Southside High.

Even after getting that news, I continued to write in my journal. It felt good to get the worries off my mind and onto the page. I got so absorbed, I didn't even notice when Dad came in my room.

"What are you writing?" he asked.

I nearly jumped out of my skin. "It's . . ." I almost lied and said it was an essay for English class. Because writing in a journal is kind of embarrassing. But something in my father's eyes made me tell the truth. "It's a journal.

My English teacher said writing things down would make me feel better."

Dad tilted his head, curious. "Does it?"

I shrugged. "Yeah, it kind of does."

Dad looked thoughtful. "The doctors at the V.A. hospital said I should write a journal. Maybe I'll give it a try."

So Dad got his own "scribbling notebook." He sat in the room with me. For a while, the only sound was the scritch-scratching of our pens on paper.

Then Armi bounced in and asked, "What are you doing?"

We both slapped our notebooks shut and said, "Nothing."

Then Dad winked at me, and we both laughed.

Later, Dad said, "You know, Benny. I think your teacher is right. Writing helps a little."

I put down my pen and took a deep breath.

"Dad," I mumbled, "I'm sorry. I shouldn't have run away."

Dad shook his head. "I'm sorry I drove you away. But at least we're together again."

CHAPTER 19

On Friday afternoon, Steve said, "Coach Wunderman is hoping you'll be able to play on Squad Night. He says the soccer squad needs you."

My head felt completely normal now, unless I pressed right on the wound. I knew I was up to playing, but . . .

My eyes darted across the living room to Dad. He had just come home with a shopping bag.

Dad must have seen the panic in my face, because he said, "Don't worry, *mijo*. I'll stay home tomorrow night. The docs say it might be a while before I'm ready for crowds." Then he added, "But they did recommend playing soccer with this."

He reached in the bag and pulled out a bright pink soccer ball. "The docs thought I might get over my phobia if I started playing with a ball that doesn't look like a soccer ball."

I smirked. "You mean we're going to practice with Barbie's soccer ball?"

Steve laughed. So did Dad. Then he said, "Let's give it a try!"

No one had to ask me twice. I was sick of playing sick around the house. I couldn't wait to get outside and kick a ball—even if it was as pink as Barbie's Dream House.

THWACK! My foot met the ball at just the right angle. Dad blocked it and passed to Steve. He kicked it to me. I kicked to Dad.

And there was this wonderful feeling of everything being okay again—at least for a while.

Chapter 20

Mom thought I ought to stay home on Squad Night. "If you stayed out of school this week, you shouldn't be playing sports on Saturday."

But Dad stuck up for me. "The coach is counting on Benny. Besides, he's fine. You should have seen him kicking the Barbie ball all over the lawn this afternoon."

The pink ball had the same effect bowling shoes used to have. Just the mention of it made us laugh.

Mom shrugged. "As long as you're feeling okay, I guess it's all right."

"I'm better than okay," I said. "I'm in the pink!"

Armi groaned. "If you keep saying things like that, you won't be for long!"

But I was superfine at Squad Night. It was like my feet had wings! I barely noticed my sore head. And in the short game against the football team, I scored more points than Rob.

Turned out none of the football guys had been on steroids after all. But they still said they were "off their game" because of the testing. Ha! They weren't off theirs. We were just on ours!

Best of all, nobody called me Camel Spider.

When the night was over, Coach Wunderman put his arm around my shoulders. He bragged to Mom, "Your son is an excellent athlete. If he keeps practicing the way he has been, Benny could qualify for a college scholarship."

Mom beamed. "We're all very proud."

Some of the guys from the soccer squad were going out to celebrate. But Mom said, "Come on, Benny. We have to get home."

I wished I could have gone with the rest of the squad. But I didn't want to spoil a great evening by arguing with Mom.

As soon as we opened the door, I knew why Mom was so eager to get home. The smell of homemade enchiladas greeted us like a warm hug.

Even better was the sound of Dad's voice joyfully singing, "Deep in the Heart of Texas." He rushed out of the kitchen to ask, "How was Squad Night?"

Armi grinned. "Benny was the star!"

I blushed and said, "Not really. But the soccer squad totally creamed the football team—even worse than last year. And I scored more points than Rob!"

Dad smiled. "Then you were the star!"

I smiled, too. "Teamwork. That's what Coach Wunderman says." Then my stomach growled. "Are the enchiladas ready?"

Dad nodded. "They'll be on the table by the time you wash your hands."

I pity anyone who's never had homemade enchiladas. They're the best! And Dad's beans are much better than the ones you get in restaurants because he doesn't mush them too much. So they're chunky, not just a smooth paste.

I was glad Dad cooked enough for leftovers. Because I could eat that meal every day!

CHAPTER 21

I knew our troubles weren't over. Dad still had his camel-spider moments. But they weren't so often, and I no longer wanted to run away.

I didn't feel so hopeless anymore. In fact, I felt like I had something to say. So when Mrs. McCormack assigned an essay on any topic, I wrote about "The Effects of PTSD on Soldiers' Families."

I got an A-minus—and a smiley face.

That was something new for me, since English had never been my best subject. But I started thinking that I might even become a reporter.

One day, during English class, I drifted into a daydream. I pictured myself as a journalist embedded in an army unit.

I was there when the soldiers invaded a terrorist cell. And I wrote an award-winning human-interest story about how the unit saved a group of kids playing soccer. The soldiers dismantled a land mine that was planted dangerously close to one of the goals.

The kids cheered. Their parents cheered. My boss cheered. "Bravo, Benito!"

"Benito!" Mrs. McCormack's voice interrupted my triumphant daydream. "Didn't you hear the question?"

"Huh? Wha . . . ?" I stammered.

Mrs. McC sighed and said, "Please see me after class."

I blushed so much my ears got hot.

After the bell rang, I apologized to Mrs. McCormack. She asked, "What were you thinking about when you should have been focusing on English class?"

"Well, I actually was thinking about writing," I said. Then I explained about my daydream of being an embedded reporter.

Mrs. McCormack smiled. "Becoming a reporter is a fine goal. I'm glad you want to develop your writing skills. Now just try paying more attention in class."

I nodded. But the truth is, I was already daydreaming again. If the war was over by the time I graduated, maybe I could become the first reporter to be embedded in a professional soccer team. That job would really be a kick!

About the Author

Justine Fontes and her husband, Ron, hope to write 1,001 terrific tales. So far, they have penned more than 600 children's books. They live in a quiet corner of Maine with three happy cats.

SOUTHSIDE HIGH

ARE YOU A SURVIVOR?

check out all the books in the

SURVIVING SOUTH SIDE

collection.

Bad Deal

Fish hates having to take ADHD meds. They help him concentrate but also make him feel weird. So when a cute girl needs a boost to study for tests, Fish offers her one of his pills. Soon more kids want pills, and Fish likes the profits. To keep from running out, Fish finds a doctor who sells phony prescriptions. But suddenly the doctor is arrested. Fish realizes he needs to tell the truth. But will that cost him his friends?

Recruited

Kadeem is a star quarterback for Southside High. He is thrilled when college scouts seek him out. One recruiter even introduces him to a college cheerleader and gives him money to have a good time. But then officials start to investigate illegal recruiting. Will Kadeem decide to help their investigation, even though it means the end of the good times? What will it do to his chances of playing in college?

Benito Runs

Benito's father had been in Iraq for over a year. When he returns, Benito's family life is not the same. Dad suffers from PTSD—post-traumatic stress disorder—and yells constantly. Benito can't handle seeing his dad so crazy, so he decides to run away. Will Benny find a new life? Or will he learn how to deal with his dad—through good times and bad?

Plan B

Lucy has her life planned: she'll graduate and join her boyfriend at college in Austin. She'll become a Spanish teacher and of course they'll get married. So there's no reason to wait, right? They try to be careful, but Lucy gets pregnant. Lucy's plan is gone. How will she make the most difficult decision of her life?

Beaten

Keah's a cheerleader and Ty's a football star, so they seem like the perfect couple. But when they have their first fight, Ty is beginning to scare Keah with his anger. Then after losing a game, Ty goes ballistic and hits Keah repeatedly. Ty is arrested for assault, but Keah still secretly meets up with Ty. How can Keah be with someone she's afraid of? What's worse—flinching every time your boyfriend gets angry, or being alone?

Shattered Star

Cassie is the best singer at Southside and dreams of being famous. She skips school to try out for a national talent competition. But her hopes sink when she sees the line. Then a talent agent shows up, and Cassie is flattered to hear she has "the look" he wants. Soon she is lying and missing rehearsal to meet with him. And he's asking her for more each time. How far will Cassie go for her shot at fame?

THE PROTECTORS

Luke's life has never been "normal." How could it be, with
his mother holding séances and his stepfather working as a
mortician? But living in a funeral home never bothered Luke
until the night of his mom's accident.

Sounds of screaming now shatter Luke's dreams. And his
stepfather is acting even stranger. When bodies in the funeral
home start delivering messages, Luke is certain that he's nuts. As
he tries to solve his mother's death, Luke discovers a secret more
horrifying than any nightmare.

SKIN

It looks like a pizza exploded on Nick Barry's face. But bad skin
is the least of his problems. His bones feel like living ice. A
strange rash—like scratches—seems to be some sort of ancient
code. And then there's the anger . . .

Something evil is living under Nick's skin. Where did it
come from? What does it want? With the help of a dead kid's
diary, a nun, and a local professor, Nick slowly finds out what's
wrong with him. But there's still one question that Nick must
face alone: how do you destroy an evil that's *inside* you?

THAW

A July storm caused a major power outage in Bridgewater. Now a research project at the Institute for Cryogenic Experimentation has been ruined, and the thawed-out bodies of twenty-seven federal inmates are missing.

At first, Dani didn't think much of the news. But after her best friend Jake disappears, a mysterious visitor connects the dots for Dani. Jake has been taken in by a cult. To get him back, Dani must enter a dangerous, alternate reality where a defrosted cult leader is beginning to act like some kind of god.

UNTHINKABLE

Omar Phillips is Bridgewater High's favorite teen author. His fans can't wait for his next horror story. But lately Omar's imagination has turned against him. Horrifying visions of death and destruction haunt him. The only way to stop the visions is to write them down. Until they start coming true . . .

Enter Sophie Minax, the mysterious girl who's been following Omar at school. "I'm one of you," Sophie says. She tells Omar how to end the visions—but the only thing worse than Sophie's cure may be what happens if he ignores it.

THE CLUB

The club started innocently enough. Bored after school, Josh and his friends decided to try out an old board game. Called "Black Magic," it promised players good fortune at the expense of those who have wronged them.

But when the club members' luck starts skyrocketing—and horror befalls their enemies—the game stops being a joke. How can they stop what they've unleashed? Answers lie in an old diary—but ending the game may be deadlier than any curse.

MESSAGES FROM BEYOND

Some guy named Ethan has been texting Cassie. He seems to know all about her—but she can't place him. He's not in the yearbook either. Cassie thinks one of her friends is punking her. But she can't ignore the strange coincidences—like how Ethan looks just like the guy in her nightmares.

Cassie's search for Ethan leads her to a shocking discovery—and a struggle for her life. Will Cassie be able to break free from her mysterious stalker?